This edition published in 1990 by Gallery Books,
an imprint of W. H. Smith Publishers, Inc.,
112 Madison Avenue, New York, NY 10016

ISBN 0-8317-4914-8



Gallery Books are available for bulk purchase for
sales promotions and premium use. For details
write or telephone the Manager of Special Sales,
W. H. Smith Publishers, Inc., 112 Madison
Avenue, New York, NY 10016.
(212) 532 6600

Typeset by Best-Set Typesetter Ltd, Hong Kong
Printed and bound in Singapore

# JACK AND THE BEANSTALK

## AND OTHER FAIRY TALES

ILLUSTRATED BY RENE CLOKE

GALLERY BOOKS
An Imprint of W. H. Smith Publishers Inc.

HER BROTHERS HAD TURNED INTO SWANS

# CONTENTS

# JACK AND THE BEANSTALK

ONCE upon a time there was a poor woman who had a son named Jack. They lived in a small tumbledown house, and all they had was one cow. One day the cow stopped giving milk, so the woman told her son to take it to market.

"Make sure you sell it for plenty of money," she warned him.

On his way to market, Jack met a man who asked him if he would sell the cow.

"Only if you pay me a good price," Jack said, obeying his mother's instructions.

"I have something worth more than any

money," the man told him. "If you let me have the cow I will give you these magic beans in exchange." He showed Jack a handful of green and pink beans, which Jack thought were very pretty.

Jack let the man lead the cow away,

THE MAN GAVE JACK SOME BEANS

then he hurried back home carrying the beans safely in his hat.

"Is that you, Jack?" called his mother when she heard him come in. "Why are you back so soon? I hope you made sure you were paid enough for the cow," she added hopefully.

"Oh, yes, Mother, I did!" cried Jack, who was feeling very pleased with himself. "I met the strangest man, who offered me these magic beans. So I sold him the cow – look how many he gave me."

"Beans!" his mother screamed. "You sold our valuable cow for just a handful of silly old beans! Now we shall starve. How could you be so stupid?" She stamped her foot and shook her fist at him.

"But, Mother, they are not ordinary beans," Jack protested. "They're magic."

"Nonsense!" shouted his mother, and she snatched the beans from him and threw them out of the window.

Jack's mother was so angry that she sent him to bed without any supper. He awoke

"BUT THEY ARE MAGIC BEANS!"

early the next morning feeling hungry. To his amazement, Jack saw a gigantic beanstalk growing outside the window.

"So the beans were magic after all," he thought. "I have never seen a beanstalk even half as big before. I wonder how high it is."

He ran outside and looked up, trying to see the top. It seemed to reach way up into the clouds, so he started to climb up it. Jack climbed and he climbed and he climbed and he climbed for what seemed an age. Finally he reached the top. The clouds stretched away into the distance like a wide white road, and Jack decided to see where it would go.

Far in the distance, Jack could see a huge castle. When he reached the front door, he knocked as hard as he could.

The woman who answered was the

SO JACK CLIMBED UP IT

tallest person he had met in his life.

"What do you want?" she asked suspiciously, peering down at Jack.

"Please let me in. I think I am lost, and I am very hungry," Jack said.

"You can come in and have something to eat if you can make yourself useful," the woman said grumpily.

So Jack followed her into an enormous kitchen and ate the bread and cheese she gave him. Then she told him to get inside a huge cooking pot and start cleaning it. Suddenly they both heard the sound of heavy footsteps outside.

"Quick, you will have to hide! My husband has come home early, and he is very fierce and bad-tempered," the woman warned him.

Jack crouched down at the bottom of the cooking pot, hoping he would not be

seen. In came the most hideous giant. With a sniff, he began to chant:

*"Fee-fi-fo-fum,*
*I smell the blood of an Englishman!"*

"I expect you can smell the soup I have made for your supper," said his wife.

She put some on the table, and the giant sat down and drank it noisily.

"Bring me my money bags," the giant ordered when he had finished his meal.

THE GIANT LIVED IN A HUGE CASTLE

His wife fetched some leather bags, and the giant opened one and tipped a heap of gold coins onto the table. Chuckling greedily to himself, he began to count

JACK ESCAPED WITH THE MONEY BAG

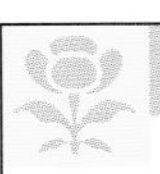

them, putting the coins back into the bag one by one. But before he had quite finished, he fell asleep at the table and sat snoring in his chair.

Jack, who had been watching from his hiding place, climbed out of the pot. Taking care not to wake the giant, he took one of the money bags off the table and quickly made his escape.

Down the long white road Jack ran, then climbed down the beanstalk. Later he could hear the giant roaring with rage above his head. It sounded just like thunder.

When Jack got home he told his mother about his adventure. She was overjoyed to have the gold but insisted he must never go near the giant again.

Some time later, however, Jack could not resist climbing the beanstalk one

more time in search of adventure.

Again he asked the woman if she needed a boy to help with odd jobs. The woman thought she recognized Jack, but she wanted to find out what had happened to the gold so she told him to come in and clean out the milk churn.

Soon after, the giant came in shouting:

*"Fee-fi-fo-fum,*
*I smell the blood of an Englishman!"*

The giant searched all around, but fortunately he did not see Jack who was hiding behind the milk churn.

After supper the giant asked for his magic hen. Jack could hardly believe his ears when he heard the giant say, "Lay, hen, lay!" and the bird promptly laid a golden egg on a velvet cushion.

As soon as the giant fell asleep, Jack tucked the hen under his arm and

escaped down the beanstalk once more.

Jack's mother praised him for being so clever. Jack was soon curious to see more of the giant and his magic. Back up the beanstalk he climbed. This time Jack did not tell the giant's wife he was there. Instead, he crept into the house without letting her see him. When the giant came

THE HEN HAD LAID A GOLDEN EGG

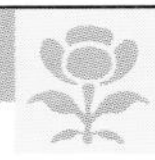

storming in, Jack hid behind the woodpile as the giant shouted:

*"Fee-fi-fo-fum,*
*I smell the blood of an Englishman!"*

His wife said, "You must be imagining it, dear. There is no one else here."

Grumbling as usual, the giant gobbled up his dinner. Then he called for his magic harp. When he said, "Play me a merry dance," the golden harp obeyed. "Now play me a lullaby," said the giant.

So the harp played, singing sweetly until the giant fell asleep. Jack came out from his hiding place and picked it up. But as he ran out of the door, the harp called out, "Master! Master!"

"Who's stolen my harp?" roared the giant, waking up suddenly. "I know it's that rascal who tricked me before. This time he will not get away."

The giant started to chase after Jack, who raced along the road and climbed down the beanstalk as fast as he could. The giant was following him, but Jack reached the bottom first and rushed into

the house to fetch an axe. With one mighty stroke, Jack cut right through the beanstalk. The giant fell to the ground with a terrible crash, banged his head on the ground and died instantly.

Jack and his mother lived very happily after that. Every day, the hen laid an egg made of pure gold, and the harp sang and played for them. But Jack never went in search of adventure again.

THEN JACK CUT DOWN THE BEANSTALK

# GOLDILOCKS AND THE THREE BEARS

THREE bears once lived in a little house in the wood. There was a great big father bear, a medium-sized mother bear and a little tiny baby bear.

One morning the mother bear made some porridge, and while it was cooling the bears went out to play in the forest.

While they were out, a little girl named Goldilocks found the cottage and went in. She tried to sit on the big arm-chair but it was too hard. She tried the middle-sized chair but it was too soft.

The smallest chair was just right – but

GOLDILOCKS WENT INTO THE COTTAGE

then it broke! Now she felt hungry. She tasted the porridge in the big, green bowl but it was too hot. In the middle-sized, yellow bowl it was too cold. But in the little, red bowl the porridge was just right so she decided to eat it all up.

SHE ATE IT ALL UP

Then Goldilocks went upstairs. When she saw the bears' beds, she climbed onto the biggest one but it was too lumpy. Next she lay on the middle-sized bed but it was too squashy. Finally she tried the little tiny bed, and it was so comfortable that she fell asleep. When the bears came back from their walk they soon guessed someone had been in the cottage.

"Somebody's been sitting in my chair!" growled the great big father bear.

"Somebody's been sitting in my chair!" grumbled the middle-sized mother bear.

"Somebody's been sitting in my chair – and they have broken it all to pieces!" cried the little tiny baby bear.

Then they noticed the porridge bowls.

"Somebody's been eating my porridge!" growled father bear.

"Somebody's been eating my porridge!" grumbled mother bear.

"Somebody's been eating my porridge – and they have eaten it all up!" cried poor little baby bear.

When the bears went upstairs they saw their beds. "Somebody's been sleeping in my bed!" growled father bear.

"Somebody's been sleeping in my bed!" grumbled mother bear.

"Somebody's been sleeping in my bed – and here she is!" shrieked baby bear.

Goldilocks woke up with such a fright that she leaped out of bed and ran all the way home without stopping.

THEN THE BEARS RETURNED

# THE WILD SWANS

LONG ago there lived a King who had eleven sons and one daughter called Elisa. They were very happy as children, though their mother had died.

When the King married again, the new Queen – who had magic powers – decided to send the princes away. So she put a spell on them, turning them into eleven wild white swans. Nobody knew why the princes had disappeared. All anyone saw was a flock of swans, wearing golden crowns, flying away from the palace.

Princess Elisa was sad at losing her

SHE TURNED THEM INTO WILD SWANS

brothers and spent hours wandering in the forest alone, searching for them. She thought that something had happened to them while they were out hunting.

One day Elisa wandered too far off the path and got completely lost. Further on she came to a stream. She stopped to wash her hands in the cool, clear water and have a drink. Then she heard someone coming. A little old lady came into sight, carrying a basket of berries. She gave some to Elisa and asked why she was all alone and looked so sad.

"I came looking for my eleven long-lost brothers. But now I am lost myself. Have you ever seen the princes hunting in these woods?" Elisa asked.

"I have not seen any princes in the woods," the old woman said. "But yesterday I saw eleven wild swans, wearing

ELISA STOPPED BY A STREAM

golden crowns, swimming in this stream."

Elisa was curious and hid in the bushes. Sure enough, just before sunset, the swans returned. And, as each one landed, it changed from a swan into a prince. With a cry of joy Elisa rushed to meet her brothers. They were overjoyed to see her and told her how a spell had been cast on them.

"We only change back into men at night, and we live in a far-off land now, but twice a year we can come back here," they explained to their sister.

"We always hoped we would find you again," the youngest one added.

"Please take me with you," Elisa begged.

"We could try," they promised. "But the journey is very dangerous. It takes two days to fly across the sea, and the

THE SWANS WORE GOLDEN CROWNS

only place for us to rest during the night, when we are men, is on a tiny rock far out in the ocean."

To carry Elisa, they wove a net out of reeds. Taking it in their beaks, they flew up into the clouds with her.

A storm blew up and Elisa feared they would never find the rock in the crashing waves. They reached it as the sun was setting – and only just in time, for the swans were turning into princes and tumbling out of the sky. All night long the sea pounded at the rock, but next day they flew on to the distant land.

Elisa took shelter in a cave in the woods. One night she dreamed that a fairy told her how to break the spell on her brothers. She learned that she must go to the churchyard at midnight to collect stinging nettles and trample them

THEY LANDED ON THE ROCK

into shreds. These had to be spun into yarn, woven into cloth and made into shirts for her brothers. As soon as each magic shirt touched a swan the spell would be broken. Until then she must not utter a word or her brothers would die. Elisa did all this, despite terrible stings from the nettles.

Then one day the King of this land discovered her hideout while he was hunting with his men. When he saw her, the King fell in love with Elisa's beauty.

The King spoke to Elisa but she would not answer. He was fascinated by the beautiful girl and decided he wanted her to be his Queen. He took her back to his castle and dressed her in fine silks and robes. He ordered preparations to be made for a royal wedding. But his advisors were very suspicious about the

THE KING SAW ELISA IN THE CAVE

silent girl who did nothing but spin, weave and sew green shirts all day.

One night they followed her when she went to the churchyard to collect nettles. There were other people in the churchyard at night who were up to no good, and witches often haunted the place. That night some witches were meeting together close to the place where the nettles grew.

"That girl is working with the witches," the King's advisors whispered to each other when they saw Elisa go in the witches' direction.

If they had waited they would have seen her creep past the witches.

The news was reported to the King, who was horrified. Sadly he had to order his soldiers to arrest Elisa and put her on trial for being a witch. The King was

hoping she would speak at last and tell everyone she was innocent. But still she said not a word. Her fine clothes were taken away and she was dressed in an old sack, bundled onto a cart and carried off to prison.

SHE GATHERED NETTLES AT NIGHT

However, she insisted on taking her sewing with her, which they allowed her to do, as it seemed harmless enough. Elisa had only one shirt left to finish. Could she do it in time?

The swans, who had been following her, and who understood what Elisa was trying to do, flew down onto the cart.

Just as the cart reached the prison gates, the last shirt was ready – or almost. Elisa threw the shirts onto the swans' backs. As they touched their feathers, each swan instantly changed into a prince – all except for the youngest. One of his arms remained covered with feathers, for the shirt sleeve was not quite finished.

The brothers snatched Elisa from the guards while cries of amazement went up from the crowd. The King rushed to

ELISA KEPT ON SEWING

the scene when he heard the good news.

At last Elisa was free to speak. "I am innocent!" she cried, and then the King was told the whole story.

So the wedding took place after all, and the brothers were invited as special guests. They all stayed to live with Queen Elisa in her new kingdom.

THE SWANS TURNED BACK INTO PRINCES